STICK DOG

SLURPS SPAGHETTI

By Tom Watson

SCHOLASTIC INC.

Dedicated to Michael

(65 ROSES)

ISBN 978-1-338-28202-3

12 11 10 9 8 7 6 5   19 20 21 22 23

Printed in the U.S.A.   40

First Scholastic printing, March 2018

Typography by Jeff Shake

TABLE OF CONTENTS

CHAPTER 1

CHEEZ DOODLES

Stick Dog was on his belly inside his pipe. Karen, Mutt, Stripes, and Poo-Poo all huddled closely to him. The dogs had stopped searching for food more than an hour ago. They retreated with empty stomachs to Stick Dog's pipe and positioned themselves side by side to generate extra warmth.

Karen, the dachshund, asked, "How long has it been?"

"How long has it been since what, Karen?" Stick Dog asked.

"How long has it been since we had some food?"

Stick Dog thought about it for a minute. He cast his eyes up to the gray metal ridges on the ceiling of his pipe. "It was last night. Remember? We found a bag of Cheez Doodles behind the mall."

"Ergh!" Poo-Poo snarled low and hard at the memory. "I wouldn't even call those things food, Stick Dog. They were more air than anything. You take a bite, and that orange, puffy caterpillar thing just evaporates."

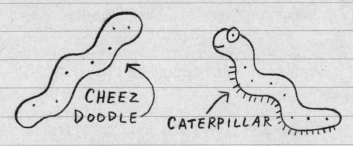

CHEEZ DOODLE

CATERPILLAR

"I agree," Stripes chimed in. "Let's not call Cheez Doodles food. Things that are more air than flavor shouldn't count."

Can I ask you something?

Wait. You remember that I can interrupt now and then, right? Yeah, it's part of our deal. I get to mention little things that

bug me or interest me. It's usually just
something from the story that gets me
thinking. So here's what I'm thinking about
right now.

What the heck are Cheez Doodles anyway?

You know what I'm talking about, right?

Those things that are puffy, curly, and really
bright orange?

How do they make those things?

I think maybe it's like popcorn. The corn
kernel starts out tiny but then blows up to
make light, fluffy popcorn.

Maybe they take a little piece of cheese,
blow it up with nuclear energy or

something, and—*Shazam!*—Cheez Doodle.

It would be awesome to work in a Cheez Doodle factory and blow up cheese every day. Plus I'd get to work with nuclear energy.

And I bet I'd get free Cheez Doodles.

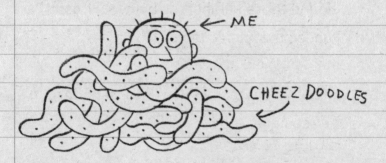

Imagine that. Free Cheez Doodles. All day.

I even like saying "Cheez Doodle."

Cheez Doodle. Cheez Doodle. Cheez Doodle.

I can eat a million of those things. You know why? Stripes is right—they are more air than food.

"Okay, then," said Stick Dog. "If Cheez Doodles aren't food, then I suppose the last time we ate was yesterday morning. We found those hamburger buns at Picasso Park under that picnic table."

Karen, Stripes, and Poo-Poo all nodded in agreement.

Mutt, however, did not. He stood up and walked a few steps away and turned his head from the others.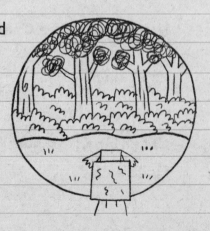

"Mutt?" Stick Dog asked. "What is it? It looks like something is troubling you."

Mutt turned his head to face Stick Dog. Then he lowered his chin and stared down at the floor of the pipe. "It's just—" he began. But he stopped himself.

Stick Dog smiled. Mutt was the largest of them all. He tended to lumber when he ran. He shook Stick Dog's pipe when he plopped down to relax. He had a deep voice and a slow, friendly way of speaking. Stick Dog suspected he was about to see another example of Mutt's sensitive side.

Stick Dog tried again. "Just what, Mutt?"

This was the final nudge of encouragement Mutt needed. He answered, "It's just that I ate something else yesterday—that you guys didn't."

"WHAT?!" Poo-Poo yelled.

"You didn't share!?" yelped Stripes.

"Mutt, oh, Mutt," Karen said. She sighed and shook her head slowly back and forth.

Stick Dog held up a paw as quickly as he could to quiet the others. He thought there was probably more explanation to come. "It's okay, Mutt," he said. "What was it? What did you eat?"

"Some rope," Mutt said, and finally turned to his friends before hanging his head again. "I found it behind the hardware store on Highway 16."

"You're the only one of us who eats rope, Mutt," Stick Dog said, and smiled. "We wouldn't have wanted any."

"You guys don't eat rope?" Mutt asked.

They all shook their heads.

"Boy, you don't know what you're missing," Mutt said. He felt better already. "Well, I'm still sorry I ate it. I wanted to bring it back so we could play tug-of-war."

"Tug-of-war! I love tug-of-war!" Karen exclaimed immediately. "It gives me a chance to show off my mighty dachshund power! Do you still have it? Can we play now? Can we?!"

Poo-Poo and Stripes thought a game of tug-of-war sounded like a fun idea too. Even Stick Dog seemed intrigued by the prospect. It would be, he suspected, a terrific distraction from their hunger.

Mutt shook his head as he answered and explained. "No, we can't play now. I ate the whole thing. I was going to bring it back, but while I carried it in my mouth, I tasted some of those loose strings on the end. You know, the frayed threads at the end of a piece of rope? I love those things. I just had to stop and chew on them. And before I knew it, the rope was gone."

"The whole thing?" Stripes asked. "There's nothing left to play with?"

"I'm sorry," Mutt said. He seemed truly sad

about the entire thing. "Sometimes, I just can't help chewing and swallowing things. It wasn't very nice of me. I could try to find another piece of rope. Maybe I have some stuck in my fur that I forgot about."

Mutt immediately began to shake, and several things—including a bottle cap, two pencils, an empty potato chip bag, and a red mitten—shot quickly out from his fur.

But there was no rope.

The disappointment on Mutt's face was clear. He felt like he had let down his friends. Poo-Poo, Stripes, and Karen were discouraged too. They wanted to play tug-of-war.

Stick Dog knew he had to do something to lift their spirits. They were all hungry. There was no rope to play with. Mutt felt terrible about eating the rope—and now consoled himself by chewing on the mitten.

"You know what?" Stick Dog declared to the group. "I don't think I've ever wanted to play tug-of-war so badly in my life. All this talk about it has made me remember just how fun it is."

He smiled and looked at his friends. He focused on Karen last.

"I bet I could beat you in tug-of-war," he said, and pointed at her.

"NO WAY!" she screamed. She hopped up and down at the challenge.

"Let's try to get another piece of rope and find out," Stick Dog suggested.

"Great idea!" Mutt declared after dropping the mitten from his mouth. "And I promise not to eat this one!"

Karen, Poo-Poo, and Stripes thought it was an excellent idea too. They followed Stick Dog, hurrying off to the hardware store, where Mutt had found that first length of rope.

Stick Dog knew his friends' attention had

already turned away from their lack of food.
What he didn't know was this: their search
for rope would lead them to something
utterly delicious.

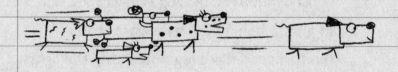

CHAPTER 2

PERFECTLY PROPORTIONED

"Okay, Mutt," Stick Dog said as they skid to a stop behind the hardware store. The sun had set. Stick Dog noted that the lights were off in the store, and he scanned the area for humans. It looked plenty safe. "Where did you find that piece of rope yesterday?"

"Right over there," Mutt answered, and pointed. "By the corner of that Dumpster. On the ground."

They trotted over to the Dumpster and looked all around. They found two bottle caps, a dented soda can, and a dried-up marker—but no rope.

Mutt tucked the bottle caps, soda can, and marker into his fur for safekeeping.

"Karen?"

"Yes, Stick Dog? What can I do for you?"

"Can you take a look under the Dumpster for another piece of rope?"

"You want me to dive under the Dumpster?"

"If you don't mind," replied Stick Dog. "I think you're the only one of us who can fit comfortably under there."

"Humph!" Karen said, and exhaled loudly. "Are you saying I'm short?! Is that what you're implying?"

Stick Dog paused a few seconds before answering. He appeared to be carefully contemplating his response.

"Not at all," he said. "I'm saying you're perfectly proportioned for this task."

"Perfectly proportioned?"

"That's right."

"Perfectly?"

"Yes."

"Perfect?"

"Correct."

Karen smiled and dove toward the edge of the Dumpster. She squished and squiggled herself past the bottom edge, squirming and squashing herself with great determination and conviction. Once past the edge there was plenty of room underneath the Dumpster. Karen was more comfortable and able to stand up.

Stick Dog, Mutt, Stripes, and Poo-Poo stood at the edge of the Dumpster waiting for Karen's report.

"Anything?" Stick Dog called after a minute.

"You were right, Stick Dog," Karen called back. "I really am just the right size for a job like this. None of you giant behemoths could fit under here."

Stick Dog grinned a bit. "That's certainly true."

"I mean, I was just looking at myself under here," Karen said proudly. "My length and my shape are quite unique. I can explore strange new places—like under this Dumpster. I can boldly go where no dog has gone before. I can fit where no other dog can fit. I'm truly an amazing canine specimen."

"You certainly are right about that," confirmed Stick Dog.

"Imagine—just imagine—if one of you humong-a-saurs tried to get under here," Karen said, and giggled. She seemed to be visualizing just such a thing. "It would be ridiculous. I'd have to pry you guys out with a crowbar."

HUMONG-A-SAUR!

Stick Dog said, "I suppose you would."

"What was the word you used?" Karen asked from beneath the Dumpster.

"When?"

"When you wanted me to come under here. When you were describing me?"

"'Proportioned'?"

"No. Something else."

"'Perfectly'?"

"That's it!" Karen yelped. "Perfect! Yessiree! I like that word, all right."

"I do too," Stick Dog said, and smiled—he

couldn't help himself. He loved how quickly Karen's mood had changed.

"Stick Dog?"

"Yes?"

"Why am I under here again?"

Stick Dog shook his head ever so slightly. "You're looking for a piece of rope. Remember?"

"We all want to play tug-of-war," Poo-Poo said, trying to help.

"I ate the last rope," called Mutt to refresh her memory.

"Oh, right. Rope," Karen said. You could

tell she was turning her head all around to
search for rope now that she remembered.
She kept bumping the top of her head
against the bottom of the Dumpster.

Stripes wanted to know how Karen's search
was going. "Anything?" she called.

"No. Nothing. Just an old Styrofoam container. I'll push it out."

"Shoot." Mutt sighed. "I really wanted to find some rope to play with. And you know, I wanted to eat it when we were done playing."

"You would eat some more rope?" Stripes asked.

"Sure," Mutt answered immediately. "It provides great chewing satisfaction—and it tastes pretty good too."

Karen used her nose to nudge the Styrofoam container all the way out from beneath the Dumpster. She squeezed out right after it.

"No rope. Just this thing," she said, and bumped her nose on the box's lid to point at it. When she did, it popped open. It happened so quickly they didn't even notice the words and picture on the lid.

All five dogs leaned down and peered inside.

They couldn't believe their eyes.

"Ropes!" Mutt exclaimed.

CHAPTER 3

SLURP-OFF

"Those are awfully skinny ropes," Stick Dog said. You could tell he didn't quite believe what he was looking at were ropes at all. "And there are only a few of them."

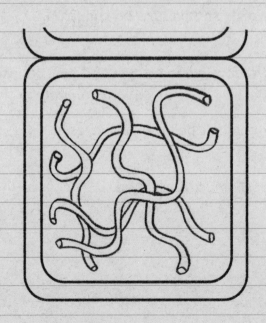

"Skinny ropes. Fat ropes. Who cares?"
Karen said. "And we only need *one* to play
tug-of-war."

Stripes said, "They're covered in red stuff."

"Red stuff. Blue stuff. Who cares?" Karen
yelped. "Let's play!"

And then, without hesitation, Karen leaned
down to get one of the long, skinny objects.
She was the shortest, after all, and didn't
have that far to reach. She wrapped her lips
around the end of one of the skinny ropes
that stuck out a bit—and pulled. It seemed
to be tangled up with three or four other
thin, flimsy strands.

Karen pulled a little harder, and the rope
seemed to loosen. Then, instead of pulling at

it, Karen sucked at it. The skinny rope splattered small splotches of red stuff and then broke free.

And disappeared.

Completely.

"Where'd it go?!" Poo-Poo asked.

They all looked at Karen.

She did a fantastic and glorious thing.

Do you know what she did?

She chewed.

And then she chewed some more.

She swallowed.

And then she smiled.

"Mutt!" she screamed. "You're right! Ropes taste GREAT!!"

That was all Stripes, Mutt, and Poo-Poo needed to hear. They all reached down, clenched a strand between their lips, and slurped.

Stick Dog waited until everyone had a turn,

then he took the final skinny, limp rope for himself.

"Whoa!" was the first thing anyone said.

It was Mutt.

"This rope tastes WAY different—and WAY better—than the rope I ate yesterday. I can't even describe how much more flavorful these ropes are."

"I can," said Poo-Poo. He then went into a trance-like stillness.

The others knew exactly what would happen next. Poo-Poo would relay his own specific thoughts and descriptions about this newfound food. They stopped chewing momentarily to listen.

"It's a stringy, starchy, scrumptious treat,"
Poo-Poo began. His nose was elevated
slightly as he pondered and spoke. "There's
a substantive, almost bread-like strength to
the strings. And there's a heartiness and
freshness to the red splotches. I'm
reminded of that glorious evening when we
discovered what pizza was. Do you
remember that tomato goodness that was
spread beneath the layer of cheese? This
red flavor is much like that red
flavor. I taste salt and pepper,
sure. But there's a deeper level
of spice and flavor here.

I get hints of oregano, garlic, and onion on the back of my palate. It's a filling, tasty, stringy delight."

Poo-Poo then lowered his head and looked at the others one at a time.

Stick Dog spoke for them all. "Well said, Poo-Poo. Well said."

With that, they licked their lips and whiskers, attempting to capture any final specks that might have splattered from their slurping.

Do you like slurping?

I do.

Do you know what a "Slurp-Off" is?

You don't?

I'll tell you.

It's a contest. Well, more like a game really.

Here's how it works.

Get some spaghetti noodles.

Cook them. You know, boil them in water.
Mom boils mine for me. Maybe one of your
parents can boil a bunch for you. Mom won't
let me boil my noodles myself—even though
I'm totally old enough. Whenever I want to
cook something on the stove, Mom says,
"Remember the flaming dish towel
incident?"

Anyway, a Slurp-Off works like this: You get a bunch of cooked noodles that are the same length. You put some tomato sauce on them. Then you get a friend and challenge them to a Slurp-Off.

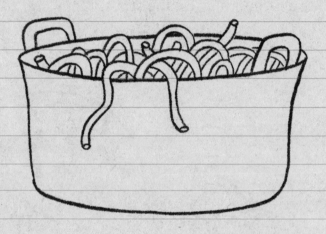

Whoever slurps the most noodles the fastest is the winner.

Now, if Stick Dog and his pals were having a Slurp-Off, they would have tied. That's because each dog got just one noodle each.

They did still get pretty messy though.

Stripes licked some of the red stuff from her whiskers and lips. A wicked and mischievous grin came to her face. She asked the others, "What's black and white and red all over?"

Mutt answered, "A zebra with a sunburn."

"A penguin with the chicken pox," guessed
Poo-Poo.

Karen said, "A banana dipped in chocolate!"

"No. No! Those are all good guesses
though!" exclaimed Stripes. She was
noticeably thrilled that everyone was so
interested in her riddle. "Stick Dog, do you
have a guess?"

He shook his head and smiled. The truth is
that he did have a guess. And he was pretty
sure he knew the answer. But he wanted
Stripes to have the chance to supply the
punch line. "Karen said what I was going to
guess."

Karen then came a step closer to Stick
Dog and winked at him. "Great minds think
alike."

Stick Dog nodded to her and then turned to
Stripes. "What's the answer? What's black
and white and red all over?"

Stripes giggled to herself for several seconds and then said, "Me!"

When Poo-Poo, Mutt, and Karen were finished groaning—and Stick Dog was finished grinning and shaking his head a bit—they looked down at the empty carton. Playing tug-of-war was now the last thing on anyone's mind.

Mutt seemed to speak for the group when he said, "We need to find some more of those skinny, flimsy ropes, Stick Dog."

"They're all gone, Mutt," replied Stick Dog. "I don't know where we'll get any more."

"That's totally unfair!" yelped Stripes. "All we get is a little taste and then it's over?!"

Stripes's frustration instantly affected the others.

"Stick Dog, why did you bring us here anyway?" Mutt asked.

"We were looking for rope, remember?"

"But we were looking for rope to play with, not to eat," Poo-Poo moaned. "Now we've got a little taste, but there's none left. That's the worst!"

"Oh, Stick Dog," sighed Karen. "It's like that time we tasted those rainbow puddles left behind from the ice cream truck. A little taste but nothing else! Totally frustrating."

"Wait a minute," Stick Dog said. He seemed bothered. It appeared that he wanted to set something straight. "Didn't I lead us to the ice cream? Didn't I almost get caught by the police? Didn't we share eleven cartons of ice cream?"

"Umm, I think you might be exaggerating your accomplishments," Karen said.

"And besides, Stick Dog, we can't live in the past," Stripes added. "We have to live in the NOW. And right NOW we need to find some more tasty ropes."

"I'd like to, Stripes," Stick Dog replied calmly. "It's just that we don't have a clue about where to start."

Poo-Poo looked down at the empty box

and slapped a paw at it in frustration.

When he did, the lid flipped halfway shut for a moment and then flapped back open. It was closed just long enough for Stick Dog to see words and a picture on top of the box.

"Wait a minute," Stick Dog whispered. He reached down and closed the box again.

Stick Dog read the words on the box out

loud. "'Tip-Top Spaghetti Restaurant.'" He cocked his head and let the words sink in. The words were above a picture of a tall hill or mountain.

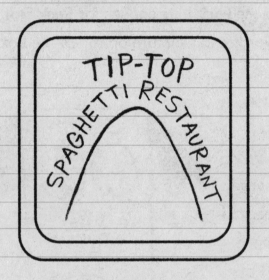

Nobody said anything. Poo-Poo, Mutt, Karen, and Stripes all watched Stick Dog closely. There was a look on his face. His forehead was wrinkled; one eye was squinted. They had all seen this look on Stick Dog before.

He was working something out.

There was suddenly a nervous energy among the group. They knew that an adventure was about to begin—an adventure that might just lead to more food.

"What is 'spaghetti'?" Karen asked.

"That must be what was inside the box," said Stick Dog.

"Not rope?" asked Mutt.

"I don't think so," Stick Dog whispered. He was still thinking.

"Well, I LIKE spaghetti!" yelped Poo-Poo. "I could eat a bunch of it!"

Stick Dog repeated the words on the box—
as much to himself as to anybody else. He
stared at the picture. He whispered, "Tip-
Top Spaghetti Restaurant. Tip-Top Spaghetti
Restaurant."

Karen asked, "What does that mean, Stick
Dog? The words and the picture?"

He answered slowly—as if he was still
figuring things out as he spoke. "There's
only one really tall hill around here," he
said. "It's past Picasso Park. I've never been
up there. Have any of you?"

None of them had.

"We're going up there tonight," Stick Dog said.

Mutt, Poo-Poo, Karen, and Stripes began jumping up and down. They trusted Stick Dog. They believed he could lead them to food.

Before speaking again, Stick Dog looked at each of his comrades with a fierce and determined gaze. "If there is spaghetti up there," he said, "we're going to get it."

CHAPTER 4

LASSOS AND TEAMWORK

"That's a really big hill, Stick Dog. How will we get up there?" asked Stripes.

Before Stick Dog could even answer, Poo-Poo said, "I know how to do it. It's easy."

You could tell Stripes, Mutt, and Karen were anxious to hear his idea about reaching the top of the biggest hill in the suburbs. They all stepped a little closer to Poo-Poo to listen. Stick Dog remained where he was.

"It's simple," Poo-Poo said. "All we need to

do is find a really, really long piece of rope, see. And we tie a big, loopy thing at the end. A lasso—that's what it's called."

"But we can't find any rope, remember? That's why we came here in the first place," Stick Dog said. But his friends didn't hear him. They were far too wrapped up in Poo-Poo's plan.

Poo-Poo continued, "Then we wait."

"What do we wait for?" Mutt asked.

"An airplane."

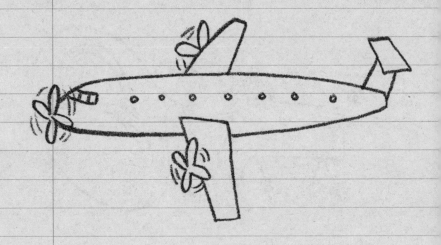

"An airplane?"

"An airplane," confirmed Poo-Poo. "When the airplane flies overhead, we throw the lasso. It wraps around one of the propellers. We hold on to the other end. The plane carries us up toward the spaghetti

restaurant. When we get there—wah-lah!—
we let go!"

"Sounds great!" Karen yelped. "Let's find
some rope!"

And with that, Mutt, Karen, and Stripes
began to search for rope even though Karen
had just, you know, searched for rope and
not found any.

"How long should the rope be to reach an
airplane, Poo-Poo?" Stripes called as she
searched.

Poo-Poo thought about it for a few seconds.
It was his plan, after all, so he wanted to give
a good answer. He called back, "At least ten
or twelve feet."

"Don't you think that's a little too long?"

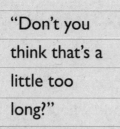

"Well, remember," Poo-Poo began to explain, "we need extra to tie the lasso at the end."

"Oh, right."

"Poo-Poo, can I ask you a question too?"

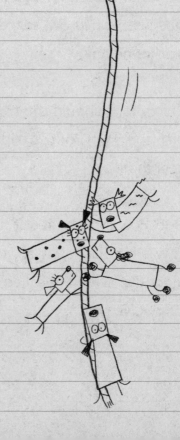

"Sure, Stick Dog," Poo-Poo said. "Although I can't think of any flaw in my plan. It's absolutely foolproof."

"When we throw that rope up to the airplane and it gets caught in the propeller," began Stick Dog, "won't the rope wind up and get all tangled?"

"Yeah, I guess so. What's your point?"

"Well, my point is, the rope will just keep wrapping around the propeller. It will get shorter and shorter—until it reaches the very end of the rope."

"Right. So what?"

"Umm," said Stick Dog. He waited, hoping he wouldn't have to ask the question. After several seconds, however, he asked,

"Where are we hanging on to the rope?"

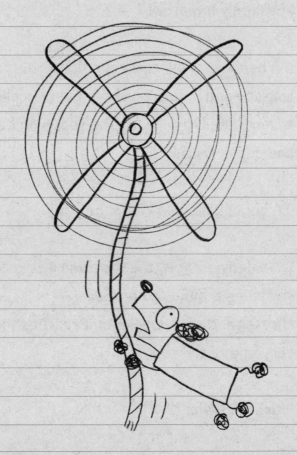

"At the very end. Obviously," said Poo-Poo.

"Why do you ask?"

Stick Dog didn't answer. Instead he waited for Poo-Poo to figure it out. And after about thirty seconds, he did. You could tell when it happened. Poo-Poo seemed to visualize the rope getting shorter and shorter as he and the others got pulled closer and closer to the propeller. He cringed and trembled when he thought of the ultimate result of his plan.

"Hey, guys," he called to Mutt, Karen, and Stripes. "I think we better stop looking for rope now. I know it's an excellent idea and everything, but, umm, I'm a little tired of coming up with excellent ideas all the time. I think one of you should get a turn for a change."

"That's very noble of you," Stick Dog said quietly.

"Yes. Yes, it is," Poo-Poo replied. Then he added, "It's just in my nature."

"Well, then," Stick Dog said after Karen, Mutt, and Stripes had gathered around him. "Do any of you have another idea to get to the hilltop?"

"I do," said Stripes as she raised a paw. "I do indeed."

"Great. What is it?" asked Stick Dog.

"Well, climbing up the hill is hard and tiring, right?" asked Stripes.

"I'm not sure it's all *that* hard. But, yes, it won't be easy; that's true," answered Stick Dog.

"Well, if it's hard and tiring, we should help each other out," Stripes said. "I call it the Teamwork Plan. We all work together."

Karen asked, "How do we do that, Stripes?"

"We take turns helping each other, that's how," Stripes said. It seemed like she was done speaking for some reason. She scratched herself behind her left ear for a moment and stretched a bit as if she was about to sit down.

Before she sat, Stick Dog said, "I'm not sure I get what you mean."

Stripes straightened back up and kind of sighed under her breath. "Frankly, Stick Dog, I'm not at all surprised that my clever and sophisticated plan might be a little difficult for you to understand. I'll describe my plan some more, but please do your best to follow along."

Stick Dog squeezed his lips together tightly. It almost looked like he wanted to say something but then decided not to. Ultimately, he just said, "I'll try to keep up."

"Here's how we do it," Stripes began. "Stick Dog, you go up the hill first."

"Okay," Stick Dog said slowly.

"Mutt, you go up next," Stripes continued. "But you don't go up by yourself. You work as a team with Stick Dog. He comes down to help you. He'll give you words of encouragement as you two climb up. He'll cheer you on a bit—that kind of thing."

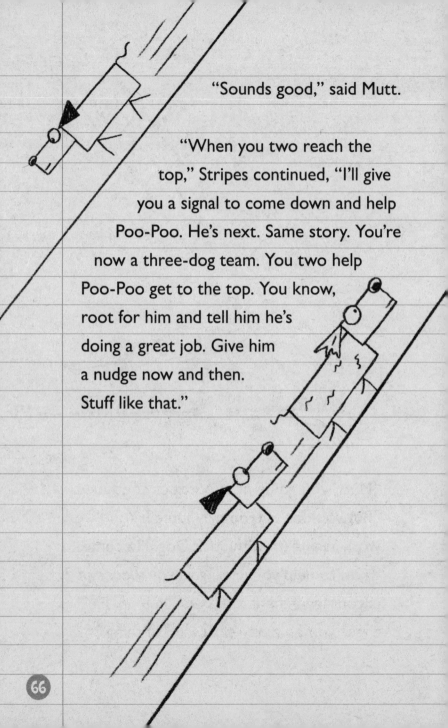

"Sounds good," said Mutt.

"When you two reach the top," Stripes continued, "I'll give you a signal to come down and help Poo-Poo. He's next. Same story. You're now a three-dog team. You two help Poo-Poo get to the top. You know, root for him and tell him he's doing a great job. Give him a nudge now and then. Stuff like that."

"Stripes, can I say something?" asked Poo-Poo.

"Certainly."

Stick Dog looked forward to this. Obviously, he figured, Poo-Poo had done the math and realized that Stripes's plan didn't add up.

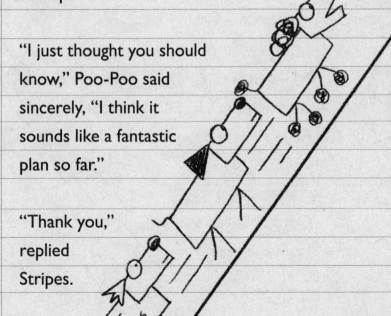

"I just thought you should know," Poo-Poo said sincerely, "I think it sounds like a fantastic plan so far."

"Thank you," replied Stripes.

She also glanced ever so quickly in Stick Dog's direction. "I'm glad *someone* here understands my most excellent strategy."

Stick Dog said nothing. He glanced up at the night sky. It almost seemed like he was trying to mentally put himself somewhere else.

Stripes then said, "Once the three of you reach the top, I'll signal you again to come down to get Karen."

"Got it," Karen said. "I join the team."

"Exactly," Stripes said. "These three will encourage you. Push you a bit. Whatever you need. Upon your arrival at the top of the hill, I'll give the final signal to come down and get me. The last trip will include all five of us—the final team!"

Mutt, Karen, and Poo-Poo all nodded their understanding toward Stripes.

Stripes herself turned to Stick Dog and asked, "*Now* do you understand how teamwork makes things so much easier?"

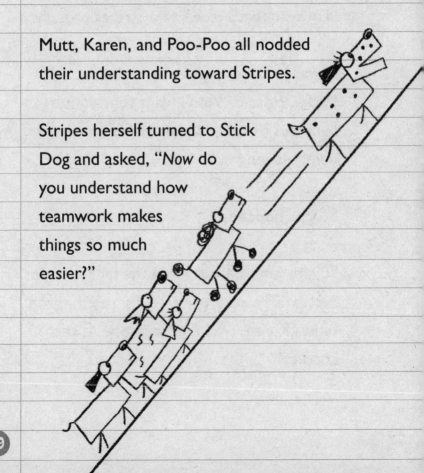

Stick Dog took a single moment to consider his response. Ultimately, he said, "It's a totally unique plan. I'm absolutely certain that I would never have come up with it myself."

"I'm sure that's true," said Stripes proudly.

"I was just doing a little counting though," Stick Dog said. "And I want to make sure I got this right. Will you double-check my numbers for me?"

Stripes nodded.

"By my count, I will go up the hill five times. Mutt will go up four times. Poo-Poo, three times. Karen, two. And you, one. Is that correct?"

"Sounds right."

"Five plus four plus three plus two plus one equals fifteen, I think," said Stick Dog.

Stripes scrunched up her face a bunch. She said, "Well, I don't have a supercomputer to do the calculations, but I believe that's correct. What's your point?"

"My point is," said Stick Dog as kindly as he could, "why would we go up the hill fifteen times when we could just go up five times— one time all together?"

Stripes didn't say anything. She shuffled her feet against the blacktop, spraying loose pebbles about. She whispered loud enough for all of them to hear, "Math is my worst subject."

"That's not your fault," Stick Dog said immediately. "It's *math's* fault."

Stripes adopted this line of thinking quickly. "It IS math's fault."

Then she growled for about ten seconds.

While she growled, Stick Dog turned to Mutt and Karen. He asked, "Do either of you have a plan to get to the hilltop to see if a spaghetti restaurant is up there?"

They both nodded and wagged their tails.

"Mine involves a hot-air balloon," Mutt said with great confidence.

"And mine requires a bonfire, a really large skillet, and five buckets of cold water," Karen said with even greater confidence.

Stick Dog cocked his head a little, trying to ensure that he had actually heard what he thought he heard. Finally, he said, "I can't wait to hear your ideas. Let's make our way over to the hill and then we can hear your plans."

"Works for me," Karen said.

"Sure, why not?" responded Mutt.

And with that, all five dogs began their journey to the tallest hill in the suburbs.

CHAPTER 5

HOT-AIR BALLOONS. CORRECTION: *STRIPED* HOT-AIR BALLOONS

It was the first time Stick Dog and his friends had ever run through Picasso Park without stopping to search for food. Karen didn't even slow down when they passed her favorite garbage can.

They ran past that garbage can. Then they motored past a swing set, basketball court, and gazebo. They exited the park on the other side and made their way across two fields, three streets, one creek, and two meadows before arriving at the foot of the tallest hill in the suburbs.

They stood in a patch of rocks and pebbles that had rolled down the hill over time. They looked up. There was, indeed, a building on the hilltop, but it was too far away to identify.

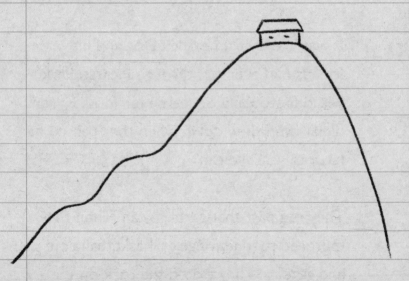

"We're never going to make it up there," moaned Stripes.

As soon as the others—well, everybody except Stick Dog—heard Stripes's doubt, they expressed similar sentiments.

"It's too far."

"I'm too tired."

"My legs hurt just looking at this hill."

Stick Dog, as you can probably guess, had a plan. He said, "It looks pretty daunting, all right. Maybe Mutt's plan can get us to the top."

Stripes, Karen, and Poo-Poo turned to Mutt with hope on their faces.

"Okay," Mutt said. "The first thing we need is a hot-air—"

Stick Dog interrupted him just then.

"Mutt, before you get started," he said, "I wonder if we could just find a better place to hear about your strategy. It's kind of rocky and uncomfortable here, and I want to settle in and really give your plan a good listen."

The others looked around on the ground, noticed the rocks and pebbles, and agreed with Stick Dog.

Mutt asked, "Where should we go, Stick Dog?"

Stick Dog looked up the hill and saw exactly what he wanted to see. There was a small plateau—a little, flat spot on the hill—about one-third of the way up.

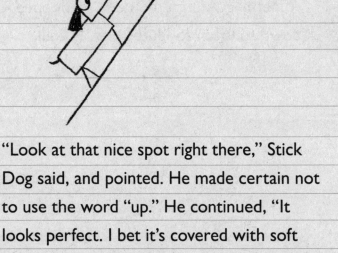

"Look at that nice spot right there," Stick Dog said, and pointed. He made certain not to use the word "up." He continued, "It looks perfect. I bet it's covered with soft grass too. Let's go there to hear your plan."

"Okay" is all Mutt said before he and the others hurried up the hill to get there. He was anxious to share his plan with the group.

Stripes, Karen, and Poo-Poo all flopped down on their bellies when they got there. Mutt sat back on his rear legs in front of them. Stick Dog scanned the rest of the hill—he appeared to be looking for something. After a moment, he flopped down to listen to Mutt's plan as well.

"Okay," Mutt said. "The first thing we need is a hot-air balloon."

"Wait a minute, wait a minute," Stripes said immediately.

"What is it, Stripes?" Mutt asked.

"This whole hot-air balloon thing," she said.

"Yes. What about it?"

"I was wondering if it could be one of those

really cool striped balloons," she said. "You know, my name is Stripes, and the balloon would be covered in stripes. I just think it would be neat. Is that okay?"

"Sure," answered Mutt, happy to oblige.

"Excellent!" Stripes yelped.

"Okay. So we get this hot-air balloon. And then—"

"*Striped* hot-air balloon," reminded Stripes.

"Right, right," Mutt acknowledged. "So we get this *striped* hot-air balloon. Then we all climb into the basket thing. The hot-air balloon soars over the top of the hill, and we jump out. Then it's spaghetti for everyone!"

"Great plan!" Poo-Poo said with terrific enthusiasm.

Karen and Stripes endorsed the hot-air balloon strategy as well.

Stick Dog asked, "Where exactly do we get the hot-air balloon, Mutt?"

"You mean *striped* hot-air balloon," Stripes corrected.

"Excuse me. Of course," Stick Dog said quickly. "Where do we get the *striped* hot-air balloon?"

"Oh, we just grab one when it floats by," Mutt answered with complete confidence. "Those things fly by all the time. You can't throw a rock around here without hitting a hot-air balloon."

"Oh, I see."

Karen then threw a couple of rocks.

She didn't hit a hot-air balloon.

"What if one comes by that *isn't* striped?" asked Stripes. "I'm not getting into just *any* hot-air balloon."

"No worries," Mutt reassured. "We'll wait for a striped one."

"Excellent!" Stripes said. She got excited about the prospect all over again.

They were all up off their bellies now. They scanned the darkening sky for hot-air balloons. Mutt kept saying things like "There should be one any second now" and "Anybody see anything? I don't want to miss one."

After a couple of minutes, Karen screamed, "I saw one!"

"Where?!" Mutt, Stripes, and Poo-Poo shouted in unison.

"I just got a glimpse of it!" Karen said. "Behind that big cloud. Where the moon was a minute ago!"

This comment caught Stick Dog's attention. He asked Karen, "The moon isn't where it was a minute ago?"

"No. Now there's just a big cloud there," Karen answered. "The cloud the balloon is behind."

"What color was the balloon?" asked Stick Dog.

"Kind of grayish-yellowish-whitish," Karen answered. "And really bright. Like it was glowing or something."

"Did it have stripes?" asked Stripes.

"Not that I remember, I'm sorry to say," said Karen. "It had, like, faded irregular-shaped spots or something, I think. Remember, I only got a quick glimpse."

"Maybe it has stripes on the other side," offered Mutt.

This idea lifted Stripes's spirits considerably.

Mutt, Karen, Stripes, and Poo-Poo stared at that cloud and waited for the hot-air balloon to emerge.

And waited.

Then it happened.

The edge of a circle appeared as the cloud slowly slid aside. It was just as Karen had described: grayish-yellowish-whitish, bright, and marked with faded, irregular spots of several sizes.

Stick Dog watched and listened.

"Karen!" yelped Poo-Poo.

"What?"

"That's not a balloon!" he exclaimed.

"What is it then?"

Mutt, Poo-Poo, and Stripes all screamed the answer at the same time.

"It's the MOON!"

Then they all started laughing.

Karen shook her head and stuck her chest out in defiance. She said, "Maybe it's a hot-air balloon that's *shaped* like the moon."

Stick Dog decided to step in then.

"It's the moon, Karen," he said definitively but kindly. "It's an honest mistake."

Karen hung her head. "That's really embarrassing."

"You know what might make you feel better?" asked Stick Dog.

"What?"

"If you shared *your* plan with us."

"What plan?" Karen asked. She was still quite dejected. Her head hung low; her tail didn't wag at all. It just drooped.

"Your plan to get to the top of the hill."

"Oh, right," she said, and lifted her head. She seemed suddenly happier. "It's a pretty nifty plan! And totally feasible. I know it will work easily."

"Before you tell us," Stick Dog suggested, "let's move away from this place. That darn moon is taunting us. It just looks so much like a balloon. Why don't we get out of here?"

"I'm with you," Karen said gladly—and then took a brief second to scowl at the moon high in the sky.

"What about my plan?" asked Mutt. "What about searching for a hot-air balloon? There's bound to be one soon."

"We'll keep an eye out," Stick Dog said quickly. "Don't worry. As soon as we see one, we'll put your plan into action."

"Sounds good."

"Where are we going, Stick Dog?" asked Poo-Poo.

"Let's just move to that next little flat area," Stick Dog said casually. He nodded his head toward another plateau farther up the hill. And before anyone could question his motives, he started walking toward the new spot.

Without thinking about it, Mutt, Stripes, Poo-Poo, and Karen followed after him.

CHAPTER 6

A GIANT SKILLET

"This looks like a good spot," Stick Dog said, and settled into a comfortable listening position. He casually glanced up the hill to see how far from the top they were.

They were pretty close.

After the others got comfortable, Karen provided the details of her own plan.

"Okay," she said, and paced slowly in front of her pals. "We need three things—and three things only."

She stopped and tapped her front left paw against the grass-covered ground three times. She said, "We need a huge skillet, a bonfire, and five buckets of cold water."

"Sounds interesting so far," Poo-Poo commented.

Stripes added, "Yes, it does."

Mutt turned his head left and right and said, "No hot-air balloons yet. But I'll keep looking."

Stick Dog nodded at all these comments but did not say anything himself.

"My plan is so simple," Karen said with substantial pride in her voice. "First, we need to build a huge bonfire at the bottom of the hill. It needs to be super-big. Second, we place the giant skillet on top of the bonfire and let it get super-hot. Finally, we each climb into the skillet one at a time."

"Is getting ourselves cooked part of the plan, Karen?" Poo-Poo asked sincerely.

"No, no. That would be ridiculous. Let's try to stay serious here," Karen responded. "My plan is far more practical, logical, and reasonable than that."

"Go on," encouraged Stick Dog. He wanted to keep the process moving. They were nearly to the top of the hill—although he didn't think his friends knew that. Being so close made Stick Dog want to get there even more.

With any luck, the Tip-Top Spaghetti Restaurant would be there. And with even more luck, they might be able to get their paws on some more of that spaghetti.

"Well, after we each climb into the skillet," Karen continued, "we sit down. In no time, the searing heat from that skillet will start to burn us like crazy. It will totally toast our tail ends. The scorching heat will make us jump as high and as far away as possible. We'll jump all the way to the top of the hill! *Ba-bam*! Game over! Brilliant plan, right?"

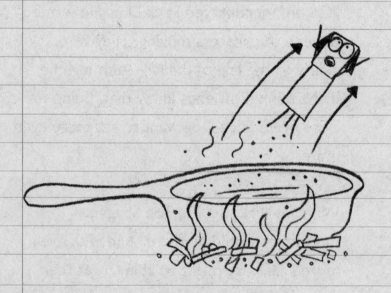

"It is brilliant," Mutt confirmed. He seemed genuinely impressed. "But what about the buckets of water? How do they come into play?"

"Oh, right. The buckets," Karen remembered. "Those are at the top of the hill. When we shoot out of the flaming-hot, sizzling skillet and land at the top, the buckets of cold water will be there to soak our burning butts in."

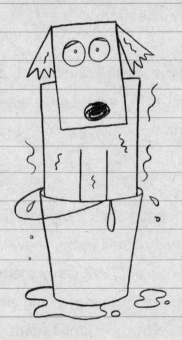

Mutt, Stripes, and Poo-Poo all agreed that this made perfectly good sense.

"Karen, I understand the bonfire and the skillet," Stick Dog said. "I just don't get the buckets."

"Umm, they're to soak our burning butts in. Pretty obvious, Stick Dog. I mean, really. Try to pay attention."

"Right. Umm, I will," said Stick Dog. "I know what they're used *for*. I just don't understand how they get to the top of the hill."

Karen looked at Stick Dog like she thought his brain had turned into a chewed-up Frisbee. She said, "We carry them up to the top before we come down and climb into the skillet. Not too complicated."

Stick Dog smiled a bit to himself. It was

pretty dark, so Karen didn't see him.

He said, "But if we carry them to the hilltop, won't we already be up there? We'll have reached our goal. We won't even need the skillet or the bonfire. Right?"

"Oh, Stick Dog, Stick Dog," Karen said slowly, and shook her head. "Where's the *style* in that? Where's the *flare*? Where's the *excitement*?"

"You mean the excitement of burning ourselves, flying through the air, and smashing back down to the ground? That excitement?"

"Exactly."

Stick Dog nodded his head. "Okay. Got it."

"I'm glad," Karen said. You could hear the relief in her voice. She was happy Stick Dog finally understood.

Stick Dog asked, "So all we need is a skillet, some buckets of water, and a bonfire, right?"

"Right."

Stick Dog looked around on the ground with great intent. He turned in every direction. His eyes scanned the ground all around. "I don't see any of those things here," he said after a minute or so of serious searching. "Let's check over that little ridge up there."

Karen, obviously happy that Stick Dog had adopted her plan, was all too willing to follow him up the hill. Poo-Poo, Mutt, and Stripes came after.

Now, as you can probably guess, the ridge was not really a ridge at all. It was actually the top edge of the hill. And in less than a minute, they were there. They stood right next to a guardrail at the edge of a parking lot.

Again, Stick Dog scanned the surrounding area to the left and to the right.

"Gosh darn it," he said. "Still no buckets, skillet, or bonfire anywhere."

Karen stood with Mutt, Stripes, and Poo-Poo close to the guardrail. They all watched

Stick Dog. They pointed at him and giggled as quietly as they could.

Stick Dog looked up.

"What?" he asked. "What's so funny?"

They all pointed at the ground and down the hillside. They shook so hard with laughter, you could barely tell where they pointed.

"We're at the top!" yelped Poo-Poo.

"What?!"

"The top of the hill!" Stripes laughed.

Mutt had tears in his eyes. "We made it, Stick Dog. We already made it!"

Karen hopped up and down. She had to catch her breath from laughing so hard at Stick Dog. When she did, she said loudly, "We reached the top! And you're up here looking for a big skillet, buckets of cold water, and a bonfire!"

Stick Dog snapped his head all around. He hurried a few steps to the edge of the hill and looked down. His eyes were opened wide, his eyebrows were raised high, and his mouth hung open.

Poo-Poo came close and put a paw on Stick Dog's shoulder. "Stick Dog, I swear," he said, still giggling, "I don't think you even know what you're doing sometimes."

Stick Dog laughed a little and shook his head at himself. It was then—and only then—that he looked all the way across the parking lot toward the building on the other side.

There was a sign on the roof. It read, "Tip-Top Spaghetti."

It was as clear, bright, and welcoming as the brightest star on the darkest night.

CHAPTER 7

A BIG PENGUIN

"It's here," Stick Dog whispered. "It's here."

"What's here?" Karen asked.

"The hot-air balloon?!" Mutt asked hopefully, and whipped his head up to scan the night sky.

"Does it have stripes?!" asked Stripes.

"No, not a balloon," Stick Dog said. "We're already on the hilltop, remember? We don't need a balloon anymore."

"Oh, right," Mutt muttered. "I forgot."

"I was talking about Tip-Top Spaghetti," Stick Dog said, and pointed with his paw. "The restaurant is right over there."

Well, this was all Mutt, Karen, Poo-Poo, and Stripes needed to hear. They had been so busy reveling in their hill-climbing accomplishment—and Stick Dog's unawareness of it—that they hadn't even noticed the building. As soon as they turned their heads and peered across the parking lot to see Tip-Top Spaghetti, their stomachs began to grumble.

GRUMBLE

A slight breeze blew the aroma of rich, thick tomato sauce toward them. They began to drool. They fidgeted nervously as they remembered the delectable spaghetti slurping they had done behind the hardware store. There was no more talk of hot-air balloons, giant skillets, and bonfires.

Now, there was only one thing on their minds—and stomachs.

It was the delicious prospect of more spaghetti.

Stick Dog put his forepaws up on the guardrail, and the others copied his action. Well, everybody except Karen. She couldn't quite reach—but she did duck her head under the guardrail to search the area the best she could. There were several cars in the parking lot, but no humans that they could see. The restaurant itself had a large window in the front next to a fancy wooden door. Thankfully, there was a row of rhododendron bushes in front of the window. They were huge and would conceal the dogs easily, Stick Dog thought.

"Let's get to those bushes," Stick Dog said. "We'll take a peek in that big window, see what's inside, and maybe we'll get a spaghetti-snatching idea."

Everyone agreed this was a good plan.

They moved across the parking lot in spurts and starts. In just a couple of minutes, they dove safely beneath the bushes by the window. The dogs scooted on their bellies until they were directly under the window.

"Careful now," Stick Dog whispered. "We'll just peek over the bottom edge and see what's inside."

What they saw made them even hungrier. At table after table throughout the restaurant,

humans sucked and slurped on giant bowls
of spaghetti.

"Humans are so strange," Poo-Poo
whispered, and stared.

"Why?" Mutt whispered back.

"Shh," Stick Dog said. "Everybody down.
Back under the bushes."

Once they were gathered and hidden safely
among the branches and brambles, Poo-Poo
answered Mutt's question.

"It's just weird the way humans eat, that's
all," he said. "It makes no sense."

"How so?" asked Stripes.

They were all interested in Poo-Poo's opinion. And while there wasn't a whole lot of room beneath the rhododendron bushes, there was enough to gather awkwardly close to Poo-Poo to listen. That's what Mutt, Karen, and Stripes did. Stick Dog, however, moved stealthily about, poking his head in and out of the bushes in different areas, trying to gather as much information as he could.

"Think about it," Poo-Poo went on. "First they push those metal things into their mouths. One has prongs on the end, and the other has a little circle."

"I think those are called forks and spoons," Stick Dog said as he passed on his way to another lookout spot.

"Whatever they're called, it's gross," continued Poo-Poo. "Why would you put metal in your mouth. On purpose?!"

"Humans do put metal in their mouths, it's true," said Karen. She seemed to be thinking of things she'd seen in the past. "Not just forks and spoons either. I've seen humans—usually smaller humans—who have metal wires all over their teeth. It's like they're in there permanently or something. So strange."

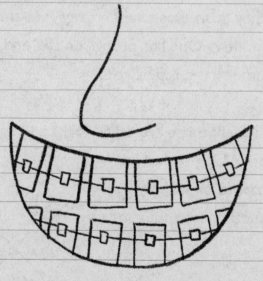

"And did you see how far away the food was from them?" Poo-Poo asked. He seemed to be slightly agitated. It was like he was offended by the way humans ate or something. "That's the way they always eat. They put the food far away on a table, then they stab it with one of those so-called forks or spoons, then they bring it up to their mouths, and it disappears. It's bizarre, I tell you."

"Why is that so bizarre?" asked Mutt.

"Because the food is only close to their noses for a split second, that's why," answered Poo-Poo a little more loudly. He was getting a bit worked up.

"Shh," Stick Dog said as he scooted by to look out of the bushes from another area.

"Lower your voice, please."

Poo-Poo continued in a whisper. "Half the fun of eating is smelling. Everybody knows that. But humans never use their noses during eating. The way we do it is so much smarter and so much more satisfying. Our noses are shoved right into the food as we eat. We *combine* the smelling and chewing experience into one all-encompassing super-sensory eating extravaganza."

"That's right; we do!" exclaimed Mutt.

Poo-Poo closed his eyes a little and lifted his chin ever so slightly. He said, "It's just one more reason why we are more advanced than humans."

They were impressed with Poo-Poo's observations. Stripes spoke for them all when she said, "You make a lot of really good points."

"There's one more thing too," Poo-Poo said. He wasn't quite done.

"What is it?" asked Karen.

"You're not going to believe it."

"What?!"

"Shh," Stick Dog repeated. "A little quieter, please."

"When they're done chewing and swallowing, they do the worst thing imaginable," Poo-Poo answered. He paused for a dramatic second or two. Then he said, "They wipe a cloth across their mouth to clean up the extra food."

"You've got to be kidding me," Mutt said, and shook his head.

"It's true. All true," Poo-Poo said, and nodded. "They wipe the best part of the meal away. Those final crumbs and drips that we get to taste over and over again throughout the day whenever we want, they *wipe them all away* without a thought. It's like they don't even know what their tongues should be used for."

"That's nuts!" Stripes exclaimed.

"Now, I will say this," Poo-Poo added. He seemed to be finishing up. "Little humans use the cloths a lot less often than bigger humans. I've noticed that. They tend to leave a little food on their faces like us. I think it's because the little ones are smarter. I think as humans grow bigger bodies, their brains shrink. The smaller ones are clearly more intelligent than the bigger ones. This whole face-wiping thing helps prove that."

"You think smaller humans are smarter than bigger humans?" Karen asked, seeking confirmation. She seemed to like this idea of little things being superior to larger things—for obvious reasons.

"Yes, I think so," said Poo-Poo. "It's just a theory. I'm not a botanist or anything."

As Poo-Poo wrapped up, Stick Dog came back. He was ready to report his findings.

"Bad news," he said. "I've looked around here a good bit. I don't see any way to get into that building to find more spaghetti. The door is way too busy. There are humans going in and out all the time."

Stick Dog was about to continue when he was interrupted by something.

There was a sound.

A rumbling sound.

It wasn't one of their stomachs this time.

It was an engine.

A big engine.

They all heard it. And it got closer.

"Maybe it's a delivery car," Poo-Poo said quickly. There was true hope in his voice. "Like the one we snatched the pizza from."

"Maybe," Stick Dog said. "But this engine sounds too big for a car. It sounds more like a truck."

"Maybe it's an ice cream truck!" Karen yelped. "Remember the ice cream truck?"

Both were things Stick Dog didn't want
his friends to think about right now. That
pizza was one of the best things they ever
tasted. That ice cream last summer had
been scrumptious. And thinking about
them would make their hunger even more
extreme. He was about to remind Karen
that ice cream trucks are only out during
the daytime and probably don't go to
restaurants anyway—but he didn't have to.
Because just then the engine sound roared
right past the bushes, stopped a few seconds
later, and went silent.

Without a word, all five dogs poked their
heads out of the bushes to see what was
happening.
They saw a
huge, burly
man step

out of a large truck. He walked toward the front door.

Before the big man got to the door, another man came out from the restaurant. He was dressed in black pants, a white shirt, a bow tie, and shiny black shoes.

"Look at that huge penguin!" Karen exclaimed. "What's he doing here? Everybody knows penguins only live at the equator. He must be lost."

"That's not a penguin," Poo-Poo said. "It's a human dressed like a penguin."

"Oh."

"Shh," Stick Dog said, and

shook his head a little. "Let's listen."

"Where do you want the linens tonight, Steven?" the truck driver asked.

"Better take them to the back door," the man from the restaurant answered. "We're too busy tonight to bring anything in the front."

The man nodded, pivoted, and returned to his truck.

Without saying a word, Stick Dog motioned his friends to duck back under the bushes. When they got there, Poo-Poo was the first to speak.

"Bummer," he said in a sad voice. "It wasn't a delivery car."

Karen added, "Or an ice cream truck."

"You're right," Stick Dog said. "It wasn't a delivery car. Or an ice cream truck."

He looked at his friends one at a time, holding his stare for a single second with each of them.

Then he smiled at them all—and said just one thing.

"But there is a back door."

CHAPTER 8

BITE, CHOMP, AND CHEW

Stick Dog poked his head out of the bushes and watched the truck move around the far corner of Tip-Top Spaghetti. The man from inside the restaurant stayed outside for a few minutes. He looked at his cell phone, retied his shoes, and stared up at the sky. It was a beautiful night.

Karen nudged her nose out from the bush and asked Stick Dog, "What's taking Penguin Man so long? Doesn't he know we have to follow the truck?"

Stick Dog was about to answer but didn't need to. That's because right then, the front door opened and someone called, "Steven, table thirteen wants you."

The man exhaled slowly and hurried back into Tip-Top Spaghetti.

"Bye-bye, Penguin Man," Karen called in a whisper once the man was inside. "I hope you find your way back to the equator!"

Stick Dog looked down at Karen, smiled at her briefly, and asked, "Can you get the others? It's time to move."

In fifteen seconds, they were on their way to the back door. They moved out to the parking lot behind the first row of cars, which provided excellent cover. Stick Dog didn't want them to be seen by humans from the big glass window. Darting from behind one parked vehicle to another, they made their way quickly to the corner of the building. There were no windows on this side, so they sprinted unseen.

From there, they watched the delivery truck pull away down the driveway. There were some empty cardboard boxes across the drive, and the dogs settled in behind them to look at the back of the restaurant. With the boxes and the darkness, Stick Dog thought it was a decent place to hide.

There was one door at the back. It was illuminated by a single lamp that hung from the wall. A cone of bright light shone down, but the rest of the area was dark. There were no windows, other doors, or anything else at the back of the building. It was simply a long brick wall with one door.

"This isn't going to be easy," Stick Dog said.

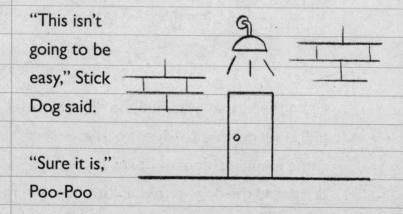

"Sure it is," Poo-Poo

stated with supreme confidence. "I got this."

And with that he began to walk toward the door. He appeared absolutely sure of himself as he strode forward.

"Poo-Poo!" Stick Dog called.

Poo-Poo stopped about halfway across the driveway and looked back at Stick Dog. "Yes?"

"What are you doing?"

"I'm going to the door," Poo-Poo explained casually. "The spaghetti is inside there somewhere. Remember?"

"Yes, I remember," Stick Dog said slowly. "But what are you going to do at the door?"

"I'm going to knock on it," Poo-Poo explained. "I've seen humans do it. One human knocks on the door, then another one opens it up from the inside. Simple."

"So, umm, you think they'll just let you in?" asked Stick Dog.

"No, don't be silly," Poo-Poo said. "I have a different idea."

"What is it?"

"When the door opens, I'm going to bite the human right on the knee," Poo-Poo answered calmly. "While they're writhing around in pain, I'll check the place out for some of that tasty spaghetti."

Stick Dog had heard enough. "Okay, thanks for explaining. But I'm not sure that's the best idea. Why don't you come back here, and we'll talk about it?"

Poo-Poo shrugged his shoulders and slowly returned to his friends. He sat down behind a cardboard box and looked at Stick Dog. He waited for further explanation.

"It's not very nice to go around biting humans, for one thing," Stick Dog began. "I mean, I know they're weird looking and strange and everything. And I know we don't trust them all that much. But I really don't believe biting them is the way to go. I also think that if you bite a human, it will scream and bring other humans. We'll be found out for sure."

"What if I don't bite, per se?" Poo-Poo asked. He seemed to be seeking a compromise.

"What do you mean?"

"What if I just chomp on them a bit?"

"Chomp?"

"Chomp," confirmed Poo-Poo. "You know; I won't bite down quite all the way."

"No. Still not very nice."

"Chew?" asked Poo-Poo. "Could I chew on a human?"

"Umm, no."

"Gnaw? How about a little gnawing action?"

"No."

"Nibble?"

Stick Dog shook his head. "I don't think your mouth should come anywhere close to a human."

Poo-Poo was silent then for several seconds. Another idea took a little time to form in his mind. Eventually, he figured it out and asked, "What if I just chewed a little piece off but then gave it back?"

"A little piece of a human's leg?"

"That's right."

Stick Dog shook his head. He looked at Karen, Mutt, and Stripes to see if they were listening. He hoped maybe they could help Poo-Poo understand that biting humans was a bad idea. But they were busy. Stripes and Mutt were taking turns putting an empty box on top of Karen and then taking it off again. Karen was giggling.

Stick Dog turned back to Poo-Poo in an attempt to convince him some more.

But he didn't have to.

Because right then something happened
that grabbed all their attention.

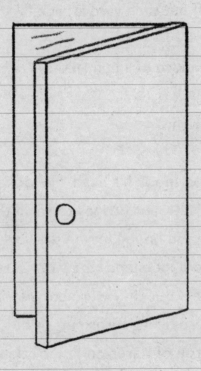

The back door opened.

CHAPTER 9

PENELOPE LOVES JOHNNY

As soon as that back door cracked open, the dogs ducked and dove behind the empty cardboard boxes across the driveway. Quickly—and safely—concealed there, they peeked out.

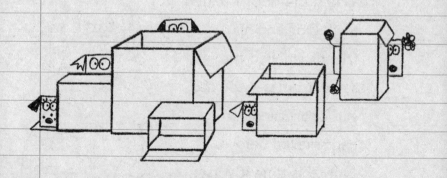

They saw one thing—and smelled another.

What they saw was a young female human step out through the doorway. She wore black pants and a white button-down shirt. She leaned against the door to keep it open. She looked behind herself as soon as she was outside, jerking her head over her shoulder to see back inside Tip-Top Spaghetti. As soon as she snapped her head around again, she plunged her hand into her pocket, snagged her phone, and began to press buttons furiously.

When the door opened, Stick Dog and his friends smelled the same aromas—tomato, garlic, oregano—they had smelled before. Only this time it was different.

Way different.

Those aromas—those delicious, hearty, mouth-drooling aromas—were stronger, thicker, and more tantalizing than before. Those scents seemed to pour out through that back doorway in great waves of scrumptiousness. They didn't even need to sniff. The smells washed over them.

"Stick Dog?" Mutt whispered.

"Yes?"

"We have *got* to get some more spaghetti!"

"Like, now!" said Stripes.

"Or even sooner!" added Poo-Poo.

Karen nodded rapidly in agreement.

"Okay," answered Stick Dog. "I'm working on it. Let's see what this human is doing."

The girl had her phone to her ear. She tapped her left foot quickly against the pavement. Then instantly her expression changed from nervousness to absolute delight.

"Hi, Crystal! It's Penelope!"

There was a slight pause and silence, then she spoke again.

"Guess what? Johnny called me, like, five minutes ago. He left me a voice mail! OMG! I just had to call my BFF!!"

Another pause.

"I know, right!? Like, OMG, I've only been waiting fifty years for him to call! But I'm totally not into him or anything! Gross. But maybe. I don't know. YOLO!"

Then a different human voice—a male voice—yelled out through the doorway.

"Penelope! Order up! Table seven!"

In a super-fast whisper, she said, "Oh, I have to go. Call you back ASAP. I'm at work! I snuck out. I'll call you right back. TBC. I have to deliver some spaghetti to this guy. He's totally cute! TTYL!"

The girl pressed a button on her phone, shoved it into her pocket, rushed back inside, and the door swung slowly—very slowly—behind her before closing tightly.

BFF! [CRYSTAL]

Stick Dog saw that the door operated with a large sprocket and hinge at the top. It kept the door from slamming shut. It helped the door close slowly, evenly—and securely.

When the door was closed, Stripes said what all of them were thinking.

"What a wack-a-doodle! Did you hear how she talked? All those letters! What's that about? What's an 'OMG'?"

"I don't know. The letters must stand for something, I guess," Stick Dog said quickly, and changed the subject. "Did you guys smell that spaghetti when she opened the door?"

This question did exactly what Stick Dog hoped. Immediately, his friends forgot about what "OMG" might stand for and focused their minds—and stomachs—on those delicious aromas. There was a warmth and heartiness to the smells.

There was something else too. There was another smell in the air. Stick Dog couldn't quite put his paws on it. It was a heavier scent. It conjured memories of that day when they ate hamburgers in Picasso Park so long ago.

He stopped trying to pinpoint that smell—and that flavor. He remembered what that female human had said. He had precious little time.

"That girl said she'd come back quickly," Stick Dog said with urgency in his voice. "I have an idea to make that door ajar when she goes back inside the next time."

"A jar?" Poo-Poo asked.

"That's right, ajar."

"What's going to be in the jar, Stick Dog?" Karen asked.

"Will there be spaghetti in the jar?" added Stripes.

"And how exactly do you plan to make the door into a jar?" Mutt asked. "Is there some sort of spaghetti magic trick you have in mind?"

"No, no. Umm, sorry," Stick Dog said as calmly as he could as he turned to make sure the door hadn't opened yet. It hadn't. "'Ajar' just means slightly open."

"I get it, I get it," Poo-Poo said. "You guys just don't know as many words as Stick Dog and I, that's all. What Stick Dog is saying is that he's going to turn the door into a jar with his special spaghetti magic trick—and the lid to the jar will be slightly open so we can eat all the spaghetti inside."

"Oh, it all makes sense now," said Karen.

Mutt and Stripes nodded their understanding as well.

"No, umm, that's not quite it," said Stick Dog. "Forget the whole jar thing. I have a plan to keep the door—"

"If we forget the whole jar thing," Stripes interrupted, suddenly distraught. Then she asked, "Where will we find the spaghetti?! It was going to be *inside* the jar!"

"There's no jar," Stick Dog said. He was trying to figure out the best way to move things along. "Umm, I don't know what I was talking about. I'm sorry. My fault."

"Stick Dog," Karen said sincerely. "You should really try to get hold of yourself. You seem very confused all of a sudden. You're getting doors and jars mixed up. You didn't even know that we reached the top of the hill earlier. And it took you quite a while to grasp the simplicity of my plan before. I mean, climb into the skillet, burn our butts, soar to the top of the hill—pretty easy stuff. Yet you didn't seem to recognize the simple genius of it all."

"You're right," Stick Dog said to Karen. He knew he had to hustle. "I'm just a little out of it, I guess. But right now we need to hurry. That girl is—"

"The one that talks funny?" asked Poo-Poo.

"The one who's all lovey-dovey, kissy-face

about Johnny?" asked Karen.

"Don't be disgusting," Stripes said.

"Right, the one that talks funny. Umm, the one who was talking about Johnny," Stick Dog confirmed. "I think she's going to come back out any minute to talk on her phone again. When she does, we'll be ready."

This was all Mutt, Karen, Poo-Poo, and Stripes needed to hear. They saw the serious look on Stick Dog's face; they heard the determination in his voice. They smelled the spaghetti in the air.

"What are we going to do, Stick Dog?" asked Mutt.

"You guys hide behind these boxes. When

the girl comes out, I want you to knock a couple of them over." As he gave instructions, Stick Dog stacked two boxes up on two other boxes. "Knock these over. It will make some noise, and she might be startled by it. If she is, she'll hurry inside. And I'll run in from the corner of the building—I'll be watching the whole time. I'm going to put something little in the way so the door won't shut. It will be ajar. I mean, umm, it will be slightly open."

Nobody said a word. They understood their instructions—and they were ready for action.

"This is our one chance," Stick Dog said. "If we can keep that door from closing all the way, we'll have a chance to get in there and snatch some more spaghetti."

Karen, Mutt, Stripes, and Poo-Poo nodded their heads. Their eyes narrowed. Their faces were chiseled with a clear sense of purpose.

"When you see her," Stick Dog reiterated— he wanted to make certain they understood his instructions—"knock those two boxes down."

They dove behind the boxes.

And Stick Dog sprinted to the corner of the building.

He peered around that corner and watched the door. In just a couple of minutes, the same girl came back. She pressed some buttons on her phone quickly and jerked the phone up to her ear.

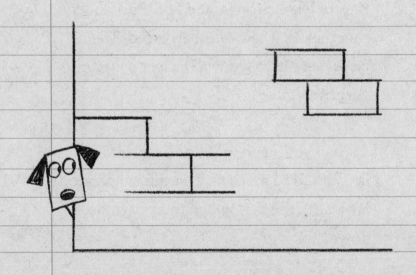

"Crystal, it's me! Your BFF!"

Stick Dog watched the boxes across the driveway, waiting for them to tumble down.

"I just listened to Johnny's voice mail! He was all, like, 'Do you know the homework for math class? LOL!'"

There was a pause in the girl's conversation. Stick Dog waited for the two boxes to fall.

They didn't.

"Math homework! P-lease, girlfriend!" Penelope said, and laughed. "I know he's not calling for homework! More like he's totally into me!"

Stick Dog knew the boxes would fall any

minute. He looked down on the ground
and found a nice-sized rock. He picked it up
with his mouth. It was the perfect thing to
drop by the doorframe to keep the door
from closing.

He stretched his legs, readying himself
to race along the building as soon as the
human ran inside.

He waited for the boxes to fall.

They didn't.

"Do you think Johnny's cute? I do! LOL! Do you think I should call him back? Or should I be, like, *whatevs?*"

Stick Dog stared at the boxes. There was no movement whatsoever.

He waited.

And waited.

The boxes did not fall.

NOT MOVING

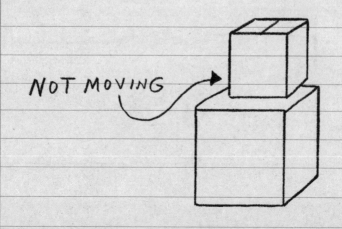

As Stick Dog stared, a deeper male human voice came roaring out through the back doorway of Tip-Top Spaghetti. It was the same one they had heard minutes before.

"Penelope! Order up! Table eight!"

Stick Dog understood instantly that the girl would go back inside quickly. He moved from the corner of the building. He took several slow steps. It was very dark out, and the girl was standing in that lone cone of light. He didn't think she would see him as

he crept closer. He took one quiet step after another, inching his way to the doorway—and the human.

"Gotta go, Crystal! Another order! We're busy tonight! TTYL!" the girl said into her phone, and pressed a button to turn it off.

Stick Dog stalked closer to her.

Closer to her.

Closer.

If she glanced in his direction, she would see him. There was no doubt.

There was a sharp stone at the edge of the building. And Stick Dog's left forepaw found it. It pierced his paw pad and sent a cold

streak of pain up his leg. He opened his
mouth to yelp but used all his energy to
stifle the sound. He succeeded. But the
rock he held dropped from his mouth—
C-Clunk!—onto the driveway and tumbled
away.

The young female human began to turn her
head and squint her eyes to see what had
made that sound.

Stick Dog knew he was caught.

CHAPTER 10

HIDE-AND-SEEK.
CORRECTION: HIDE

On hearing that rock hit the pavement, the girl began to turn her head to peer into the darkness—to peer right at Stick Dog.

He held perfectly still.

Then a second sound rang out—before she turned her head all the way to face him.

Ding!

"A message!" the girl said, and snapped

her head down to look at the phone in her hand. She stared at it as she walked through the doorway. "It's from Johnny!"

She didn't look up as she stepped inside.

The door swung slowly back to close.

But it didn't close all the way.

Because Stick Dog got there just in time.

He shoved his right paw between the door and the doorframe. The door closed on his paw.

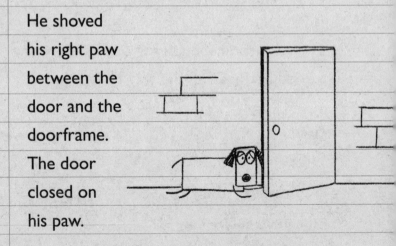

It was heavy. It wanted to be shut. With each passing second, it squeezed a little bit harder.

Stick Dog called as quietly as he could to his friends. "You guys! Over here!"

After several seconds, Mutt, Karen, Stripes, and Poo-Poo stuck their heads out from behind the boxes.

"What are you doing, Stick Dog?" Karen called back.

"My paw's stuck in the door," Stick Dog whispered loudly. "Could you guys come here, please?"

They emerged from their hiding place and trotted toward Stick Dog.

"Why's your paw stuck in the door?" asked Stripes.

"I thought you were going to use something else to keep it open," Poo-Poo said as he neared the situation. "Using your paw is not very sneaky. I don't know if you know this or not, but the rest of your body is attached to your paw. Somebody inside could see you pretty easily."

"I know that, Poo-Poo," Stick Dog said as calmly as he could. "I wasn't planning on using my paw—it just happened that way. I was going to use a rock, but I dropped it."

"Why'd you drop it?" asked Stripes.

"I stepped on a really sharp rock, and I opened my mouth to yelp. And the rock fell out," Stick Dog answered quickly. He turned to Mutt and asked, "Can you shake something out of your fur to prop the door open, Mutt? So I can get my paw out."

Mutt began to shake.

"How could you step on the rock when you were carrying it in your mouth, Stick Dog?" asked Karen.

"I didn't step on that particular rock," answered Stick Dog. "There were two rocks."

"You should really watch where you're stepping," Poo-Poo said. "Nothing hurts more than stepping on a sharp rock."

"I can think of one thing," Stick Dog whispered as the door continued to squeeze his paw.

"What's that?" Poo-Poo asked.

But Stick Dog didn't answer.

That's because right then a long screw sprang from Mutt's fur.

"Will this work, Stick Dog?" Mutt asked.

"It's perfect," Stick Dog said. You could hear real gratitude in his voice.

"Can you slide it in the crack, and then I'll slide my paw out and the door will remain ajar—I mean, umm, slightly open."

"Of course, Stick Dog."

And that's exactly what Mutt did. In just a few seconds, Stick Dog was released. He scooted out of the light a bit and rested against the restaurant's long brick wall. Karen, Poo-Poo, Stripes, and Mutt gathered around him as he attempted to rub the soreness from his paw.

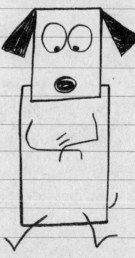

"What happened to you guys?" he asked. "You were supposed to knock over those boxes and startle the girl. When she ran inside, I was going to sprint in without being seen and prop the door open."

"You wouldn't believe how much fun we were having with those boxes," Poo-Poo said without even a hint of guilt in his voice. "It turns out empty boxes are great to have when you're playing hide-and-seek."

"You were playing hide-and-seek while I was waiting for you to knock the boxes over?"

"That's right," Poo-Poo said, and explained. "Since we couldn't play tug-of-war earlier, we thought hide-and-seek might serve as a dandy substitute."

Stripes added, "We also thought a quick

game of hide-and-seek would be a good way to burn some time until that strange-talking girl came out again. Smart idea, right?"

"Umm, sure," answered Stick Dog.

"Well, guess what?" Poo-Poo asked.

"What?"

"We forgot to pick an 'it.' You know, the one who does the seeking is called 'it,'" Poo-Poo said, and chuckled a bit to himself. "So on the count of three, we all just hid and nobody tried to find us. We were all in or under or behind those boxes the whole time."

"Until we heard you calling, that is," added Karen.

Stick Dog didn't say anything for a moment. Frankly, he didn't know what to say.

"But no harm done," Poo-Poo concluded. "The door is open now. Everything worked out great. Just great."

"You're right," Stick Dog said, and continued to rub his paw. The pain was just now starting to subside. "No harm done."

He got back on all fours and took three quiet steps toward the door.

He peered through the open crack. He turned his head over his shoulder and looked at his four friends. He said just one thing.

"I can see the spaghetti."

CHAPTER 11

PLOP

Stick Dog took almost a full minute looking through that crack. He saw a couple of humans moving about briskly. He waited until they left before inviting his friends to the door to take a look.

Mutt, Stripes, Karen, and Poo-Poo bumped and nudged their way to the doorway until they could all see inside. Stick Dog backed away so they could have a little more room.

He described what they looked at as they scanned the room from that sliver of seeing space.

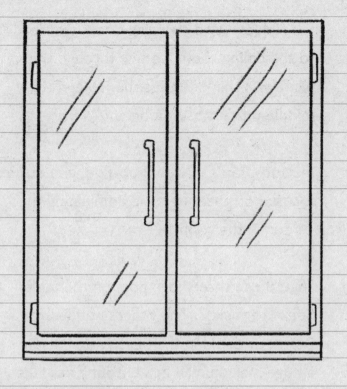

"It's the kitchen for the restaurant," Stick Dog explained in a low voice. He recalled everything he had just seen while the others looked inside. "To the left there are two big stoves. To the right there's a huge refrigerator. It's silver and shiny like a mirror. Straight ahead past the table in the middle is a sink and two swinging doors that lead to the dining room we saw through the window, I think. But it's the table in the middle that's most important."

Instantly, Mutt, Karen, Poo-Poo, and Stripes focused on the long table dominating the center of the room.

"See those three huge pots on the table?" Stick Dog asked. The others nodded the best they could in the tight space. "I saw a huge male human in a big puffy hat take stuff from the pots and put them on a plate. One pot is full of spaghetti. And one is full of the red, saucy stuff that tastes like pizza."

"What about the third pot?" asked Mutt. "What's in that one?"

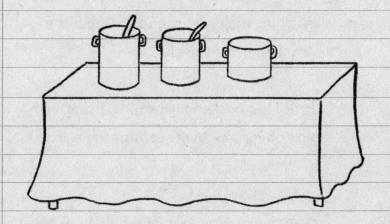

"I'm not sure. He didn't take anything out of that one," Stick Dog answered. "Okay, come back here, please. That's enough time at the door."

The group gathered in a circle around Stick Dog then. They had seen their target: the pots on the table.

"I think we can get in there pretty easily," Stick Dog said. "I've only seen two humans go in and out of the kitchen. There's the really big male and then Penelope, the strange-talking female."

Stick Dog cocked his head to listen. He didn't hear anything—or anyone—in the kitchen.

"We're going to go in and hide under that table in the middle of the room," Stick Dog said, and turned back to his friends. "It has that long cloth on it hanging over the sides. It will be a good hiding space."

"When do we go?" asked Mutt.

"Now," answered Stick Dog.

He took three steps to the door and peered inside to ensure again that nobody was there.

There wasn't.

He listened for human footsteps.

He heard nothing.

Stick Dog pushed the door open and held it for his friends. They rushed inside and dove under the table. He then stepped in himself and allowed the door to ease shut until it hit the screw. It remained open just a crack. He ducked under the table with the others.

And just in time too.

Because right then a huge man with an enormous stomach came into the kitchen through the swinging doors that led to the dining room. He wore a puffy hat and talked to himself.

"Last order of the night," he said. He had a deep, forceful voice. "One spaghetti marinara. And one spaghetti con polpette."

The table was long and wide. There was plenty of room for the dogs to hide safely.

The huge man came toward the table. The dogs could all see him from beneath the tablecloth, which almost reached down to the floor. The man's black shoes stopped right at the edge—right in front of Karen's nose.

"Spaghetti marinara," the big man said above them. The table vibrated a bit, and Stick Dog tilted his head to listen and concentrate. He heard the huge human put a plate down and scoop spaghetti onto it.

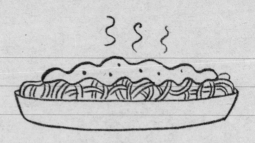

Stick Dog recognized the sound of those noodles slipping and sliding against each other. Then Stick Dog heard the sound of that red pizza-tasting sauce pour over the spaghetti. Some of that sauce spilled as the man poured it. Stick Dog heard a few big drips fall and splat on the floor and on the man's black shoes. It seemed like a very sloppy process.

"And spaghetti con polpette," the man said.

Stick Dog heard a repeat of the previous

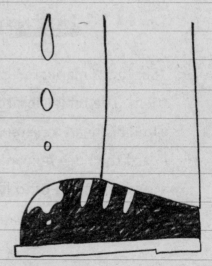

sounds. A plate was set down, spaghetti was scooped onto it, and red sauce was poured over the spaghetti.

But there was another sound this time.

A sound that Stick Dog had not heard before.

PLOP!

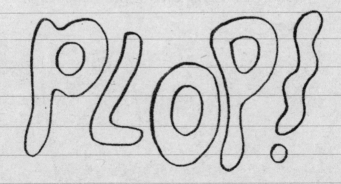

It was as if something was dropped onto the spaghetti and red sauce.

Stick Dog turned to see if his friends had heard the same plopping sound.

When he turned to them, Mutt, Stripes, and Poo-Poo were all staring at Karen. Their mouths were open in utter shock. They couldn't believe what they saw.

And neither could Stick Dog.

Karen was licking one of the giant human's shoes.

CHAPTER 12

TASTY SHOES

Stick Dog instantly forgot that plopping sound.

He knew it was all over. All their food adventures. All the good times with his buddies. Poo-Poo's obsession with squirrels. Karen's relentless tail chasing. Mutt's shaking. Stripes's crazy plans. All his friends' crazy plans, for that matter.

Everything.

Done.

Karen licked some more.

The sound came from above again.

PLOP!

There was no way Karen's shoe licking
would go undetected. Five dogs were under
the table. The door to the outside was
barely open. Even if they made a run for it,
they couldn't *all* get out the door quickly—
one or two of them might make it if they
were lucky.

Karen licked some more.

Stick Dog couldn't grab Karen. Or talk to her. He had to remain perfectly quiet—and perfectly still. Detection was certain if he made a sound or movement.

Karen stopped licking.

She scooted her little dachshund body to the left and began to lick the giant man's other shoe. Mutt, Stripes, and Poo-Poo gawked at her. So did Stick Dog.

And Karen licked.

And licked some more.

After several seconds—which felt like several years to Stick Dog—Karen took her final lick and ducked her head back under the table.

PLOP!

Stick Dog couldn't believe it.

How had Karen not been seen?

He thought about the huge human. The way he sounded. The way he walked. The size of him. The shape of him.

Size.

Shape.

Size and shape.

And Stick Dog figured it out. The man didn't catch Karen because he never saw her. He couldn't see past his own belly down to the floor.

Stick Dog closed his eyes. Absolute relief rushed over him. But it only lasted a few seconds.

Because right then the man called out, "Penelope! Order up! Table five!"

Stick Dog listened as the doors to the dining room swung open. He heard lighter, faster footsteps enter the kitchen.

"Table five, Chef?" she asked.

"That's right," he answered, and sighed. The chef sounded tired. "Last customers of the night."

Stick Dog listened as Penelope picked up the final two plates.

"I'm going to get some fresh air for a few minutes," the chef said. "We'll clean up in a bit. It's been a long night."

"Okay," Penelope said as the doors swung shut behind her.

The chef exited the door that led outside.

As soon as he did, Stick Dog emerged from beneath the table. He clenched the edge of the tablecloth in his mouth and pulled. By tugging firmly and consistently, Stick Dog moved the pots closer and closer—inch by inch—toward the table's edge.

Mutt, Karen, Stripes, and Poo-Poo came out from under the table too.

"Stick Dog?" Karen asked after observing him for a few seconds. "Why are you eating the tablecloth?"

Stick Dog couldn't answer because he was

busy and because, you know, there was a wad of tablecloth in his mouth.

"He's not eating the tablecloth, Karen," Stripes said, and snickered. "He's playing tug-of-war with it. Remember how he said he wanted to play tug-of-war so much?"

"That's right. He did," confirmed Poo-Poo.

Mutt decided to join the conversation then. "I think Karen's right," he said. "I think he's eating the tablecloth too. Sometimes things made from cloth can be quite delectable."

This thought seemed to remind Mutt of something. He gave a quick shake, and the red mitten fell from his fur. He started to chew on it.

"I still think he's playing tug-of-war," Poo-Poo said.

"But he's not tugging against anyone," Karen retorted. "To play tug-of-war, someone has to be on the other end."

This was an excellent point, and Poo-Poo and Stripes seemed to acknowledge it. They pursed their lips and nodded their heads a bit.

"Maybe he's confused," Stripes suggested. She was unwilling to concede completely. "Stick Dog is always getting confused."

Now, this debate might have gone on a while longer, but something happened right then.

Stick Dog unclenched himself from the tablecloth. He shifted his mouth left and right to loosen his jaw muscles.

"Stick Dog?" Karen said. "Can I ask you something?"

"Of course," Stick Dog said. He glanced at the swinging doors that led to the dining area. "But can you ask it quickly? We're kind of in a hurry here."

"Why are we in a hurry?"

"Umm, the humans are coming back soon," Stick Dog answered. "We have to get the spaghetti as fast as we can."

"The spaghetti!"

"Shh!" whispered Stick Dog.

"I forgot all about the spaghetti!" Karen exclaimed in a much softer voice.

"Me too!" Stripes and Poo-Poo said in unison.

Mutt tucked the red mitten back into his fur. He came closer to Stick Dog and asked, "How are we going to get to the spaghetti on top of the table, Stick Dog?"

"We don't need to get to it," answered Stick Dog. "It's coming to us."

Karen, Stripes, Mutt, and Poo-Poo tilted their heads in confusion. They stared at Stick Dog. Stripes asked the one question they all had on their minds.

"How?"

"Like this!" Stick Dog said, and smiled. He stretched up on his back paws, propped himself up at the table with his front paws, and gripped the handle of the first pot with his mouth. He could reach it now. With a gentle tug, it began to tilt. And with that tilting momentum and a little extra tug, it tipped over on its side. The rim overhung the edge of the table by a few inches.

A great mass of noodles fell to the floor.

While Mutt, Karen, Stripes, and Poo-Poo
stared in shock at the pile of spaghetti,
Stick Dog tipped the second pot in the
same manner. In seconds, a giant puddle of
red sauce accompanied the noodles on the
floor.

Stick Dog said just one thing.

"Dig in!"

And they did.

Now, eating a pile of noodles—and a
puddle of tomato sauce—off a kitchen floor
may not sound too appetizing to you.

But that's to you.

To the dogs, it was absolutely delicious.

They slurped at the noodles and lapped at
the sauce. Even Stick Dog nudged his way
into the crowd to take some bites. But he
was still curious—very curious about that
third pot. He began to reach up to tip it
over like the first two. He *had* to know what
was inside.

He stretched up toward the table.

And then he stopped.

Do you know why?

I'll tell you.

He noticed that Karen was not getting
her fair share of food down on the floor.
She kept getting nudged out of the way by
the others. It wasn't mean-spirited or on
purpose. Mutt, Stripes, and Poo-Poo were
just too focused—and too hungry—to
make room for her.

"Karen," Stick Dog said.

"Yes?" she whispered in frustration.

"Hop up on my back," Stick Dog said,
and stooped down a little. He had fallen
back to all fours paws again. The third
pot would have to wait. "You're perfectly

proportioned for another job."

"I am?"

"You are."

"What job?"

Stick Dog nodded at the two tipped-over pots on the table. He could see there were still some remaining noodles and sauce in them. Their contents had not all fallen out.

"You have to finish off everything in the pots."

Karen couldn't see inside them like Stick Dog could. She was far too short. But she could understand what this job meant: a portion of spaghetti and sauce all to herself.

In less than one second, she hopped onto
Stick Dog's back. And she was up onto
the table in even less time than that. She
pushed herself into the noodle pot first.

The pile of noodles was rapidly disappearing
from the floor—and so was the puddle of
sauce. Stick Dog decided to get a few more
slurps for himself while there was still some
left.

For one full minute, the dogs ate loads of
spaghetti and tomato sauce. They dipped

the spaghetti into the sauce. They slurped and chewed and smiled as that delicious and hearty spaghetti filled their bellies. Karen exited the noodle pot and entered the sauce pot. She licked the inside clean and savored every bite—and every drop.

While Stick Dog ate, he remained constantly alert for anyone to come back into the kitchen.

Nobody did.

It worked out nicely that Karen stepped out of that second pot right when the others were almost finished licking the floor. She hopped down to Stick Dog's back and then to the floor to join them.

While his friends got the last splotches of red sauce off the floor, Stick Dog propped himself up on the table like before and used his nose to push the pots back toward their original positions. It wasn't hard—the pots were empty now.

He raced to the other side of the table and tugged on the cloth cover again until the pots were back in the center of the table.

He took one look at that third pot—one quick, hard, curious look.

And that's when he heard footsteps—heavy footsteps—coming from outside. He heard pebbles scatter and scratch across the pavement.

The chef was returning.

"Under the table, now!" Stick Dog yelped as loudly as he thought he could without being detected. He ducked back under the table from his side, while Poo-Poo, Mutt, Karen, and Stripes ducked under from their side. He motioned for everyone to be still and quiet. He laid his head flat against the floor and peeked out at the door.

The chef came back into the kitchen. The door closed on the screw, but he didn't seem to notice. It remained cracked open just a bit. The chef took two steps toward the table.

And stopped.

"Chef?" a voice called as the doors swung open.

"It's Penguin Man!" Karen whispered.

"Shh!" said Stick Dog.

"Table three wants to give personal compliments to the chef," Penguin Man said. "Can you come out?"

"Yes," the chef answered. "I don't mind

waiting to start cleanup, that's for sure."

And with that, both humans left the kitchen.

Stick Dog couldn't believe it. The coast was clear.

"Okay, guys. Out. Now!" Stick Dog said quietly but forcefully. He held the tablecloth up so the others wouldn't snag themselves on it. Stripes and Mutt pushed the door open and exited. Karen and Poo-Poo followed.

Stick Dog took one look at that third pot. He considered investigating it but decided the risk was too great. He pivoted to head outside just when the door squeezed shut.

All the way shut.

The long screw that held the door open was gone.

Stick Dog was trapped.

And he heard human footsteps approaching.

CHAPTER 13

THE THIRD POT

Stick Dog ducked back under the table.

He was alone.

Inside.

His friends
were together.

Outside.

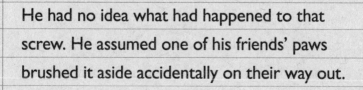

He had no idea what had happened to that
screw. He assumed one of his friends' paws
brushed it aside accidentally on their way out.

It didn't matter now. He had to figure out a way to escape.

He did not feel unsafe or vulnerable under the table. It was a good hiding place. The five of them had hidden securely under the table already, after all. Karen had even licked the huge chef's shoes undetected from under there.

No, feeling safe for the time being wasn't the problem.

The problem was, Stick Dog had no idea how he could escape. And in a few seconds, he wouldn't be alone anymore. Those human footsteps grew louder and louder.

He knew the door was heavy—his paw still ached from it. And the door was shut tightly. The only other way out was the front door. Passing through the dining room and a bunch of human customers to get to that door, which was likely shut tightly too, was out of the question.

For the first time in a long time, Stick Dog didn't know what to do. He crossed his paws on the floor and laid his head down on them. He closed his eyes to think and concentrate. There had to be a way out.

Stick Dog was already deep in thought when the doors to the dining room swung open and someone entered the kitchen. It was not Penelope or the chef.

It was Penguin Man.

He walked right over to the table. Stick Dog could see his shiny black shoes.

"These look good," the man said to himself. "And plenty of them too."

Stick Dog heard the man pull something from the third pot on the table. It had to be the third pot. Stick Dog knew the other two pots were empty—and licked clean by Karen. What was the man grabbing? Stick Dog had to know. His instincts told him he had to know. There was something important in there.

Stick Dog took a huge risk then. He pushed his head out from under the table—and suddenly he could see the whole kitchen. And he could see it safely.

From under the end of the table he stared at the shiny silver refrigerator at the far end of the room. It reflected everything in the kitchen.

Stick Dog watched.

He could see what the man grabbed, and in three more seconds he heard what the man said.

"That's a good meatball," the man whispered to himself. Stick Dog heard him chew and swallow. He watched him dig his hand into the pot again. The table shook just like before. "And one more for the road."

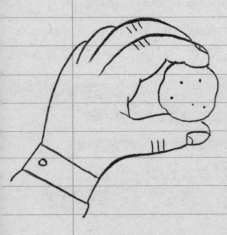

Penguin Man chewed, swallowed, and quickly left the kitchen.

"Meatballs?!" Stick Dog whispered as he ducked back under the table.

Balls made out of meat? Stick Dog could hardly believe such a wonderful, glorious, amazing thing existed. He began to salivate.

The third pot had meatballs in it.

He now had two missions: get those meatballs, and escape.

And in less than one minute, Stick Dog got his chance.

The big chef entered the kitchen. Stick Dog recognized his heavy, lumbering footsteps.

"Better get started," the chef said to himself, and came right to the table. "Hmm. These two pots are already clean. Sparkling, in fact. Ready to use for tomorrow. Penelope must have cleaned them."

Stick Dog smiled. It was Karen who had cleaned those pots—with her tongue. He listened as the chef paced around the kitchen for several seconds and then came back to the table.

"Lots of *polpette* left," the chef said. "Can save these for tomorrow."

Stick Dog heard the same sound—*plop, plop, plop*—over and over. He stuck his head out again and stared into the refrigerator's reflection. He watched the chef put the meatballs in a plastic bag one after the other.

He didn't watch anymore. There were light, quick footsteps approaching. He ducked back under the table.

It was Penelope.

"What can I help you with, Chef?" she asked.

"We're in good shape. I have the meatballs all bagged up for tomorrow, and this is the last pot," he said. He sounded relieved that their work was nearly done. "Thanks for cleaning the first two pots."

There was a moment's hesitation then.

"But, Chef, I—" Penelope began to say.

But she was interrupted.

Her cell phone rang.

"Penelope," the chef said. He sounded slightly annoyed. "You know I don't like personal calls during work."

"Sorry, I thought we were done," she said quickly. "I did, umm, clean the first two pots. Can I just take this call real quick?"

The phone rang in her pocket again. The sound seemed to amplify and echo in the big, empty kitchen.

"All right," the chef said. "Outside though. Not in here. I don't need to hear you and your BFB—or whatever you call it."

Penelope giggled and said, "Thanks, Chef!"

As she turned to go out the back door, the chef added, "Prop the door open. I don't want to have to let you back in."

And with that, two vitally important things happened.

First, Penelope went out the back doorway. As she did, she slid a metal ring on the big hinge—and the door remained open.

The second thing was just as important. The chef picked up the now empty third pot and carried it to the sink—and left the bag of meatballs on the table. Stick Dog heard his footsteps. He peeked out from under the tablecloth.

The chef turned on the water at the sink and began to scrub the pot. He was turned around. His back was to the kitchen.

Stick Dog scooted out from beneath the table. He stretched up, grabbed the plastic bag of meatballs as quickly and quietly as he could with his mouth.

The chef didn't see—or hear—a thing. The running water at the sink blocked out any other noise.

Stick Dog stalked his way to the open door.

He could hear a snippet of Penelope's phone conversation.

"Crystal! You're not going to believe it!" she practically screamed from outside the open door. "Johnny texted me! OMG!"

Stick Dog slipped outside, stepped out of that single cone of light, and escaped into the darkness of night.

CHAPTER 14

LET'S ROLL

Stick Dog worked his way carefully to the empty cardboard boxes across the driveway. He circled wide in the darkness so Penelope would not spot him and then settled in behind a large box. He remained motionless and silent there. He watched and waited until Penelope pressed a button on her phone and pushed it into her pocket. She went back inside and shut the door.

"You guys!" Stick Dog called quietly, after setting down the bag of meatballs.

It was quiet for a moment.

Then Karen called back, "Is that you, Stick Dog?"

She was under a box.

Stick Dog smiled. "Yes."

"Can you be 'it'?" asked Mutt from beneath a different box.

"We forgot to pick an 'it' again." It was Poo-Poo.

"Is it really you, Stick Dog?" called Stripes.

"Yes, it's me. Everybody come out," Stick Dog said.

Mutt, Karen, Stripes, and Poo-Poo emerged from their hiding places. They all had questions for him.

"How'd you get out?" asked Karen.

Poo-Poo asked, "Did you have to bite, chomp, chew, or gnaw any humans?"

"Did you bring any more spaghetti?" asked Stripes.

Mutt asked, "What's in the bag?"

"I'll answer all your questions," Stick Dog said with a smile on his face. He was so happy to be back with his friends. "But right now let's get away from here. Let's get back to the top of the hill where we came up."

They moved around the back corner of Tip-Top Spaghetti, along the side, and to the parking lot in front. They navigated their way across the lot, past the guardrail, and to the edge of the hill.

"Before I show you what's in the bag," said Stick Dog as his friends gathered around him, "I have to ask Karen a question."

"Yes, Stick Dog? What is it?"

"Why on earth did you lick those shoes?"

"There was red sauce on them," she answered simply. "There wasn't enough to share. And it was right in front of my face. What choice did I have?"

"Weren't you scared?" asked Stick Dog.

"Scared of shoes?" asked Karen. She clearly thought the idea was preposterous. "Why would I be scared of shoes?"

Stick Dog shook his head a bit. He understood now.

"Karen," he said kindly, "there was someone *wearing* the shoes."

"No way. There was?"

"Yes," Stick Dog said, and suppressed a laugh. "The big human with the puffy hat was wearing the shoes."

Karen's eyes popped open wide with the sudden realization of what she had actually done. "Whoa," she whispered. "I am SO brave."

Stick Dog smiled. "You certainly are."

His friends formed a semicircle around him, and he pushed the plastic bag before them.

"What is that, Stick Dog?" Mutt asked again. "Why did you bring that with you?"

"Well, I just felt so bad that we didn't get to play tug-of-war," Stick Dog said. There was something mischievous in his voice—as if he was about to spring a fun surprise on the group. His friends sensed it too.

"Come on, Stick Dog!" Poo-Poo yelped.

"What is it?!"

"I just wanted to find something we could play with," Stick Dog teased.

"What is it?!" Stripes yelped, and began to hop up and down.

Stick Dog teased some more. "Something we could share."

Karen began spinning around in a circle. "Tell us! Tell us! Tell us!"

Stick Dog placed his front left paw on a corner of the plastic bag and tore it open with his front right paw. More than a dozen meatballs rolled out onto the ground.

"They're meatballs," Stick Dog said.

"Meat!" Poo-Poo screamed.

"Balls!" Mutt yelled.

"Meatballs!!" Stripes yelped.

"Balls made out of meat!" Karen screamed. "Is this some kind of crazy dream!? Am I living in a fantasy world?! Where humans aren't strange?! Where I can catch my tail?! And where balls are made out of delicious meat?!"

Stick Dog rolled three meatballs to each of
his friends and kept the last two for himself.

There was no talk. And there was no
hesitation. The dogs devoured the meatballs
in less than a minute—the perfect dessert
to their earlier spaghetti dinner.

When the meatballs were gone, they
lounged on top of that hill for a few minutes.
They were full—wonderfully full.

"I don't want to go all the way down that hill," Stripes said after a little while. "Let's just stay here for the night."

"No," Stick Dog said. "Too many humans around here. They are finishing their meals and heading out to their cars. We should probably get back to my pipe."

The others knew he was right. They just didn't want to make the long journey home.

"I have a plan to get to the bottom," Karen said.

Instantly, Mutt, Poo-Poo, and Stripes all said
they had plans too.

"No, no," Stick Dog said quickly. "This time *I*
have a plan."

"What is it?" Karen asked.

"We roll."

His friends loved that idea. Karen rolled
down the hill first, giggling the whole way.
Her dachshund body was the perfect shape
to roll down a grass-covered hill. Stripes
went next, yelping with glee the whole time.

"I'm next," Mutt said, and positioned himself sideways at the top of the hill to begin his roll.

"Wait a minute, Mutt," Poo-Poo said. "I forgot something."

"What's that?"

Poo-Poo came closer and pulled something from his own fur. It was long and thin and reflected the moonlight when Poo-Poo held it at a certain angle.

"It's a screw," Poo-Poo said, and presented it to Mutt. "I found it on the ground by that back door. Thought you'd like to have it."

"Thank you," Mutt said, and tucked the screw deep inside his fur behind his left shoulder blade. He looked at Poo-Poo. "I love screws. I used to have one just like it. Let's roll down together."

And down they went.

Stick Dog did not say anything upon overhearing their conversation. Instead, he lifted his head to gaze at the black sky. The stars had multiplied tenfold since the last time he looked. They twinkled and sparkled above him.

And below him, his four friends had reached the bottom of the hill. Their bellies were full. They signaled to Stick Dog to roll down and join them.

And that's just what he did.

THE END.

Tom Watson lives in Chicago with his wife, daughter, and son. He also has a dog, as you could probably guess. The dog is a Labrador-Newfoundland mix. Tom says he looks like a Labrador with a bad perm. He wanted to name the dog "Put Your Shirt On" (please don't ask why), but he was outvoted by his family. The dog's name is Shadow. Early in his career Tom worked in politics, including a stint as the chief speechwriter for the governor of Ohio. This experience helped him develop the unique storytelling narrative style of the Stick Dog books. Tom's time in politics also made him realize a very important thing: kids are way smarter than adults. And it's a lot more fun and rewarding to write stories for them than to write speeches for grown-ups.